MEET ALL THESE FRIENDS IN BUZZ BOOKS:

Thomas the Tank Engine
The Animals of Farthing Wood
Fireman Sam
Looney Tunes
Bugs Bunny
Flintstones
Joshua Jones
Rupert

First published in Great Britain 1993
by Buzz Books
an imprint of Reed International Books Limited
Michelin House, 81 Fulham Road, London SW3 6RB
and Auckland, Melbourne, Singapore and Toronto

Rupert Characters™ & © 1993 Express Newspapers plc.
Licensed by Nelvana Marketing Inc.,
U.K. representatives: Abbey Home Entertainment Licensing
Text © copyright 1993 Methuen Children's Books
Illustrations © copyright 1993 Methuen Children's Books

ISBN 1 85591 2848

Printed in Italy by Olivotto

RUPERT
and the
ROPE TRICK

Story by Norman Redfern
Illustrations by SPJ Design

"Sandy Bay! Sandy Bay!" shouted the driver as the bus came to a halt at the stop by the pier. "Now, don't enjoy yourselves too much. The last bus back to Nutwood leaves at nine o'clock sharp!"

Rupert and his mother stepped off the bus, followed by Bill Badger and Algy Pug.

"This way," said Mrs Bear, leading them down the steps to the beach. Rupert and Bill followed her onto the sand and began to unpack the picnic.

"Where's Algy?" asked Mrs Bear.

Rupert and Bill looked all around, but there was no sign of him.

7

"I'm up here!" came a voice from the pier.
"There's a poster for a magic show tonight.
It says that the magician has discovered
an ancient rope trick and... Are those egg
sandwiches?"

Algy raced down the steps to join his
friends on the picnic rug.

After lunch, Rupert, Bill and Algy cleared
all the litter away.

8

"Do you think that the magician has really found an old rope trick?" asked Algy.

"No," said Bill, "he's probably invented a new one. It will be done with very fine wires and special lights, I expect."

Rupert looked up at the pier. The theatre
was at the very end. The waves were
crashing against the rocks below the
theatre. It would be an exciting place to see
a magic show!

"I'm going to walk to the end of the pier,"
he told his mother.

"That's a good idea," said Mrs Bear.
"Do you and Algy want to go, too?" she
asked Bill.

"No," said Bill Badger. "We'd rather stay
on the beach."

"There's a little cove beyond this one,"
said Algy. " We're going to explore it!"

Rupert climbed the steps up to the pier, and walked out along it. When he was half-way out, he stopped to look back at the beach. In the distance, he could see Bill and Algy running across the warm sand towards the next bay.

At the entrance to the theatre, there was a
poster for that evening's show: *Tonight! The
Great Magic Show. Doctor Sanders will perform
an ancient rope trick which he discovered in the
land of the Pharaohs!*

13

A photograph was pinned to the poster, showing a mysterious-looking man wearing a dark cloak. He was holding a coil of rope, like a sleeping snake.

Rupert was fascinated. He decided to ask his mother if they might see the show before catching the bus back to Nutwood.

He was about to run back to the beach when he spotted something right at the end of the pier. It was a telescope. Rupert put a penny in the slot and looked through the eyepiece.

In the distance, he could see the little cove which Algy and Bill had gone to explore. There they were, pottering happily amongst the rock-pools. Then Rupert had a shock. Through the telescope he saw that the sea had cut off Bill and Algy's path back to Sandy Bay. They were trapped!

Rupert walked back along the pier. He tried to think of a way to rescue his friends before the tide rose too high. Perhaps he could find a local boatman to ferry them back. He began walking faster — and ran straight into a tall man carrying a small leather suitcase.

"Can't you look where you're going?" asked the stranger crossly.

"I'm very sorry," said Rupert, "but I'm in a terrible hurry. My friends have been cut off by the tide!"

"I see," replied the man. "Well, you had better go for help — and quickly!"

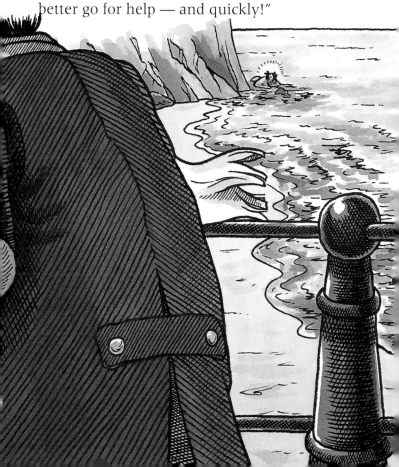

Rupert looked at the stranger again, then glanced at the picture on the theatre door.

"You're Doctor Sanders!" he exclaimed. "Won't you use your magic to help my friends? Please?"

"I'm not sure if I can," said the magician, and he frowned thoughtfully. "Wait! I have an idea. Follow me, little bear! We'll take the cliff path."

18

The man strode off along the pier, with
Rupert running behind him.

  "I don't understand," began Rupert. "How
do you think we can rescue Algy and Bill
from the top of the cliff?"

The mysterious magician smiled, and
walked ever more quickly towards the
clifftop. Rupert followed, trying his best to
keep up with the magician's long strides.

"We must make haste," Doctor Sanders
told Rupert. "The tide is in a hurry today.
See how quickly the water rises!"

Rupert looked down to the bay below.
Algy and Bill were on a tiny rock, and the
waves were coming closer and closer.

Doctor Sanders put down his suitcase and
strode to the edge of the cliff.

"Keep back," he told Rupert, "It's very
dangerous to stand near the edge."

Out of the suitcase he took a cloak as dark as night, and wrapped it around his shoulders. Next, he put on a pair of pure white gloves. Lastly, the magician took out a coil of very old rope.

"The ancient rope trick!" cried Rupert.

"Bill! Algy!" shouted Doctor Sanders down into the bay. "I'm going to throw down a magic rope. Please don't let it fall in the sea!"

Bill and Algy held out their hands as the magician threw the coiled rope down from the clifftop.

"Got it!" shouted Bill.

"Good," said Doctor Sanders. "Carefully now, lay the rope on the sand. Take the end, Bill, and hold on very tightly!"

As Bill gripped the rope, the magician recited an ancient spell. Suddenly, as if it were waking up, the rope began to uncoil. Bill held on tight as the magic rope rose from the sand, carrying him up and away from the lapping waves.

Rupert watched Doctor Sanders conjure the rope higher and higher, until Bill could step on to the clifftop.

"Well done," said the magician. "Now it's your turn, Algy!" He threw the coiled rope back down towards the bay. Once again, he spoke the strange old words, and while Algy clutched the rope, it rose to the top of the cliff.

"It really is magic!" said Bill, as he watched the mysterious man pack his cloak, gloves and rope back into their suitcase.

"Did you not believe it was?" asked Doctor Sanders. "You must come to my show tonight. Then you will see some more real magic!"

He snapped his fingers, and there in his palm were some theatre tickets.

"Three?" he asked.

"May I have one for my mother?" asked
Rupert. With a flourish, the magician
produced another ticket.

"Thank you, Doctor Sanders," said Rupert.

"And thank you for rescuing us!" cried
Algy and Bill.

"A magician must always use his magic
wisely," replied Doctor Sanders. Without
another word, he turned, and walked
briskly away along the cliff path.

That evening, before the bus left for
Nutwood, Rupert and Mrs Bear, Algy Pug
and Bill Badger went to see the Great
Magic Show.

"And now, for my final trick," announced
Doctor Sanders, "I will need a volunteer
from the audience. Ah, yes, the little bear
in the front row!"

Rupert stepped on to the stage and stood timidly in the spotlight. Doctor Sanders turned to him and whispered behind his cloak, "It wouldn't be fair for you to go home without having a go, would it?"

Then he turned to the audience. "Ladies and Gentlemen, may I present Rupert and the mysterious Rope Trick!"